LEGGS UNITED

THE PHANTOM FOOTBALLER

Alan Durant

Illustrated by Chris Smedley

Galaxy

CHIVERS PRESS
BATH

First published 1998
by
Macmillan Children's Books
This Large Print edition published by
Chivers Press
by arrangement with
Macmillan Children's Books
1999

ISBN 0 740 6084 5

British Library Cataloguing in Publication Data available
Durant, Alan, 1958-
    The phantom footballer. Large print ed. —(Leggs United ; 1)
    1. Soccer—Juvenile fiction 2. Sports stories 3. Children's
    stories 4. Large type books
    I. Title
    823.9'14[J]

ISBN 0-7540-6084-5

Printed and bound in Great Britain by
REDWOOD BOOKS, Trowbridge, Wiltshire

LEGGS UNITED
FAMILY TREE

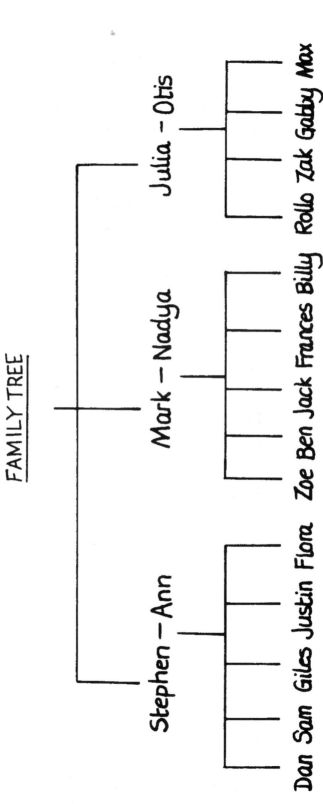

Stephen — Ann   Mark — Nadya   Julia — Otis

Dan   Sam   Giles   Justin   Flora   Zoe   Ben   Jack   Frances   Billy   Rollo   Zak   Gabby   Max

For my own super striker,
Kit Durant

CHAPTER ONE

FOOTBALL MAD

'Goal!' Sam cried. Her powerful shot bounced against the wall, between the chalked goalposts, and back to her foot. She trapped it neatly and grinned at the goalkeeper, her brother Daniel, who was now lying on the grass in front of the wall with his feet in the air.

'Beat you there,' Sam said smugly. She flicked her fringe away from her eyes. It was a warm, sunny day and her freckly face was pink from the heat.

Dan flipped himself up and shrugged. 'Your turn in goal now,' he said. He was ten, a year older than Sam and much bigger. He had a round face and large ears that he had a habit of tugging. Like Sam, and his younger twin brothers Justin and Giles, he was football mad. Next door there were more football-mad Leggs—their cousins. And yet more cousins, the Brownes, lived further down the street.

Sam wiped a bead of sweat from her forehead. 'It's so hot,' she said. 'I need a drink.'

She walked over to the wall that separated the meadow they were playing in from their garden. She pulled herself up.

'Good idea,' said Dan. 'Get me one too, will you?' He pulled at one ear thoughtfully. Even though the summer holidays had barely started, he was thinking about going back to school. This year, he'd be in the top class and in the football team. Last year, the school team had done very badly. They had let in lots of goals and lost almost every match. But this year things were going to be different. This year he would be at the centre of the team's defence . . .

There was a thump, as Sam jumped

down from the wall into the meadow. A bottle of orange drink wobbled in front of Dan's eyes.

'Your drink, master,' said Sam.

'Oh, thanks,' said Dan. He took the bottle and drank deeply. Then he burped loudly.

'Ah,' he sighed contentedly, lying back on the grass. 'I was thinking about next year,' he said, 'playing for the school team.'

Sam humphed. 'It's not fair,' she grumbled. 'I'm as good as you. I should be in the team too.' She sat down on the grass next to her brother.

Dan laughed. 'That's the rule,' he said. At Muddington Primary only children in the top year could play for the school football team. 'Anyway, who says you're as good as me?' he demanded.

'I do,' Sam replied. It was a typical Sam remark. She wasn't big-headed, she just always said what she thought.

'Well, then, if you're so good, get in that goal and prove it,' said Dan.

Sam wrinkled her snub nose. 'I didn't say I was good in goal,' she said. 'I'm better than you at scoring, though.'

'And I'm better at tackling,' said Dan.

'Oh, *tackling*,' said Sam, like she didn't think tackling was very important. She loved to run and dribble and shoot like her hero, Tommy Banks, Muddington Rovers' striker and top goalscorer. She wasn't interested in *tackling*.

'Defenders have to be good at tackling,' said Dan.

'Strikers don't,' Sam replied. 'They just have to score.'

As if to prove the point, she jumped up and whacked the ball against the wall again. The ball bounced back and hit Dan on the back of the head.

'Oi!' he cried. He sat up suddenly as if he'd been stung by a bee. 'Careful!' His pink face went even pinker.

Luckily for Sam, at that moment the twins appeared, peering over the wall. They were dressed in identical T-shirts and baseball caps. Their faces too were identical and wore the same excited expression.

'Hey, Dan! Sam!' they called as one.

'Mum and Dad are clearing out the

4

loft!' Justin cried. 'There's some great stuff!'

'They've even found an old football,' Giles added. 'Come and see!'

As soon as they heard the word 'football', Dan and Sam were on their feet. They pulled themselves up and over the wall. Then they raced across the garden towards the house.

CHAPTER TWO

THE OLD BALL

There was junk everywhere—in the hall, up the stairs, draped over the banisters. Some of it was neatly packed away in cardboard boxes and black plastic sacks. Lots more lay about in untidy heaps. Number 15 Poplar Street, where Sam and Dan lived, had been a Legg house for generations. Their dad, Stephen Legg, and his brother, Mark, and sister, Julia, had all grown up in it. Some of the stuff in the loft had been there since before they were born!

As the four siblings reached the landing, a shower of baby clothes dropped on to them from above. They shouted and, looking up, saw the big bearded face of Stephen Legg beaming down at them.

'Oh, sorry about that,' he said with a chuckle. He blew out his cheeks and wiped his forehead with one large, grubby hand. 'This is hard work,' he declared. 'My arms are aching something rotten. Is there a doctor in the house?'

'Of course there is,' Dan said. 'You.'

Stephen Legg frowned momentarily as if he'd forgotten. Then he grinned. 'Oh, yes, so I am,' he said.

'Where's the ball, Dad?' Sam asked impatiently. 'We've come to see the ball.'

'Yes, show us the ball!' cried the twins, who often said exactly the same thing at exactly the same time.

'Ah, yes, hold on a sec,' said Stephen Legg. He vanished for a few moments then, 'Catch!' he called. An object dropped out of the loft and Dan caught it.

'Is that *it*?' he said. It didn't look much like a ball. It was brown and

squashy like a baseball mitt and sort of
boat shaped. It had a big dent in the
middle with a lace in it.

'That's not a *ball*!' Sam groaned.

'Of course it is!' cried their dad. 'It's
a good old-fashioned leather ball. It's
just gone flat, that's all. So would you if
you'd been lying in that loft for over
fifty years! All it needs is pumping up
and maybe rubbing with some dubbin
to bring the bloom back to its cheeks.'

'Balls don't have cheeks!' protested

8

Justin and Giles.

'What's dubbin?' asked Dan. He was still staring at the ball as if it was a piece of old junk that should be thrown in the bin.

'It's a kind of polish,' said Dad. 'It's just the thing to put the life back into old leather. You'll find some down in the shed. You could pump some air in the ball while you're there.'

Dan looked hard at the ball. Then he looked at his dad. He seemed serious enough. 'OK, then,' he said. 'Come on, Sam.'

The shed was a big concrete hut at the bottom of the garden. It was full of bikes and tools, pots and cans and all sorts of stuff. Dan got a pump and the special valve to screw on to it, while Sam looked for the dubbin.

There was a whole shelf of different cans and plastic containers: linseed oil, varnish, wood glue, white spirit . . . She searched along the row, until, at last, she found the dubbin.

'Got it!' she cried.

'Good,' said Dan. He'd pushed the needle-like valve into a hole under the

9

lace in the ball and now he started to pump. *Clunk, hiss! Clunk, hiss!*

Sam looked at the tin of dubbin. *For making leather soft and waterproof*, it said on the lid. She opened the tin and stared at the bright apricot-coloured stuff inside. She touched it with her finger and sniffed. It didn't really smell much.

'Look, it's going up!' Dan puffed. Slowly, the ball's shape was changing. The dent was rising. After a while, the ball was full and round. Dan bounced it on the floor and then gave it a kick.

'Ow!' he said, shaking his foot. 'That hurt.'

Sam felt the ball too. 'It's really heavy,' she said. 'I wouldn't like to head that.'

'Not without a crash helmet,' said Dan.

Now that the ball was pumped up, they could see just how worn and scuffed the leather was.

'You'd better put some of that stuff on,' Dan said, nodding at the dubbin. 'You can use this.' He threw Sam an old cloth.

10

Sam took the cloth and scooped some dubbin out of the tin. Then she started rubbing it on to the ball. The leather went a little bit darker. She did the same again, rubbing harder now. She was dipping the cloth in the tin for a third time, when the shed door opened and their cousin Zak Browne came in.

'Hi,' he said pleasantly. 'What are you doing?' He was the same age as Dan and they were best friends.

'I'm putting dubbin on this old ball that Dad found in the loft,' Sam said, rubbing another dollop into the leather.

'Cool,' said Zak, pushing back a black ringlet of hair from his eyes.

'Dad says this ball's over fifty years old,' Dan said.

'Wow!' said Zak.

Sam rubbed more dubbin into the old leather, which had started to shine a little now. She wrinkled her freckly nose. 'I feel like Aladdin,' she said. She rubbed some more. 'Arise, O genie,' she moaned in a high, quivery voice that made Zak and Dan laugh. 'Arise, O genie of the ball.'

And then it happened. There was a sudden blaze of light, and out of the ball appeared a ghostly figure . . .

CHAPTER THREE

ENTER ARCHIE

Sam dropped the ball and jumped back, while Dan and Zak stood stock-still, staring in amazement at the shimmering figure before them.

It was a man with bright red hair that stood up on his head like a shock of flames. He had big bushy eyebrows and a huge walrus moustache. It was difficult to say exactly how old or how big he was, because he was sort of fuzzy and glimmered at the edges. He was dressed in a football kit in the colours of Muddington Rovers: a black and green striped shirt, white shorts and green socks. But it was a Muddington Rovers kit from long ago. The shirt had a collar and no name or words on it; the shorts were baggy and long. He wore big shin-pads under his socks and his boots were clumpy with steel toe-caps. Between the bottom of his shorts and the top of his socks two bony knees showed, so pale you could almost see through them. Round his neck, the figure wore a red knotted handkerchief like a cowboy.

'Wow!' said Sam shakily.

'Wh-who are you?' whispered Dan.

The phantom footballer stood with his hands on his hips and one foot on the old ball. In the gloomy light of the shed, he seemed to glow. He eyed the children keenly.

'Well, let us get one thing clear from the kick-off,' he said sharply. 'I am *not* a genie!' He waggled his moustache. 'Genius, perhaps.' He smiled proudly. 'My name is Archibald Legg. I *was* the inside-right and star player of Muddington Rovers. I am *now*, for my sins, a ghost.'

'A ghost?' Dan repeated.

'A ghost!' Sam exclaimed.

'Cool,' said Zak.

Sam frowned. 'But ... there's no such thing as ghosts,' she said.

Archibald Legg drew himself up and glared at Sam. His eyes appeared to fizz.

'Look, here, laddy,' he said fiercely. 'I have been squashed inside a flat football for goodness knows how long, waiting for somebody to release me. Now, at last, I am free and you say I do

15

not exist. I tell you I am a ghost as surely as you are a boy.'

His face flickered and he raised his eyebrows in a challenging look.

'But I'm not a boy,' said Sam. 'I'm a girl.'

Archibald Legg peered at Sam again. 'Of course you are, of course you are,' he muttered. 'It was just a figure of speech. The point is, I *am* a ghost and I *am* here. Now, *who are you*?'

'I'm Sam,' said Sam. 'Sam Legg.'

'I'm Dan, her brother,' said Dan.

'I'm their cousin, Zak Browne,' said Zak.

Archibald Legg appeared a little confused.

'His mum's our dad's sister,' Dan explained.

'Ah,' sighed Archibald Legg. 'Do you know, it's lovely to be amongst family.' His thick eyebrows parted like two woolly caterpillars going their separate ways. Then he smiled so that his moustache stretched amazingly. 'Now that we have been properly introduced,' he said cheerfully, 'you may call me Archie. Everyone does.'

16

'Pleased to meet you, Archie,' said Sam.

'Yeah,' Dan agreed with a big grin.

'Cool,' said Zak, who was still totally awestruck by Archie.

Archie nodded happily. 'I wonder, are there any more of you Legg and Browne lads?' he enquired.

'Oh, yes, lots,' said Dan. He did some quick mental maths. 'Fourteen,' he added. 'But we're not all lads.'

'Mmm,' said Archie. He stroked his moustache thoughtfully. 'A whole team, eh, and more?' he mused. 'I should like to meet them all,' he announced. Then he yawned. 'But right now, I think I shall take a little nap. Daylight is very tiring, you know, when you haven't been in it for so long.' His eyes blinked woozily and he seemed to slip out of focus. 'What is the date, by the way?' he asked wearily.

Dan's reply had a dramatic effect. Archie's eyes almost popped out of his head and his hair stood up even more. He quickly faded. Within seconds, he had vanished into the ball, as if sucked through the valve hole beneath the lace.

The three children looked at the ball in astonished silence, half expecting their phantom visitor to reappear. But he didn't.

'Shall we call him back?' said Sam at last.

'He said he needed to rest,' said Zak.

'Yeah,' Dan agreed. He moved forward and picked up the ball. 'Come on,' he said excitedly. 'Let's go and tell the others.'

CHAPTER FOUR

IT'S MAGIC

Ann and Stephen Legg were still busy in the loft. They were looking for things to sell on the stall Ann Legg was going to run at the following Saturday's Muddington House Summer Fair.

'Mum! Dad!' Dan called, racing up the stairs with Sam and Zak behind him. 'Come down. We've got something amazing to show you.'

Ann Legg's hot, red face appeared at the loft opening. 'Can I sell it on my stall for lots of money?' she puffed.

'No,' Dan cried. 'It's much too special for that.' He held up the ball.

19

'This old ball's magic,' he said.

Breathlessly, Dan and Sam told their mum about the ball and about Archie. She looked doubtful.

'Archie says he wants to meet you all,' Dan babbled.

'He does, he does!' Sam shouted.

Zak nodded his head in a storm of black ringlets. 'It's true, Aunty Ann,' he confirmed.

'You've got to come down and see,' Dan appealed. His large ears were scarlet with excitement. *'Please.'*

'Well, perhaps we should have a tea break,' Ann Legg said wearily.

'Put the kettle on, Dan,' said Stephen Legg.

'OK!' Dan cried. Then he, Sam and Zak tore off downstairs again.

'Mad, completely mad,' sighed Ann Legg, shaking a clump of dust and fluff from her dark hair.

'It runs in the family,' said Stephen Legg, as the twins burst past him and hurtled down the loft ladder.

*   *   *

'You know, that ball *might* be worth something,' said Ann Legg, sitting on the sofa, nursing a mug of tea. 'Perhaps we *should* sell it on my stall.'

'No way, Mum!' Dan cried in horror.

'It's you who'll benefit, you know,' Ann remarked sharply. The money raised from the stall was going to Muddington Primary, where most of the Legg children were pupils and where Zak's mum, Julia Browne, was a teacher.

'You can't sell it, Mum,' Sam said indignantly. 'It's *magic*.'

'Yeah,' Zak agreed. 'There's a ghost in it.'

'Well, that would certainly put the price up,' Stephen Legg teased. 'Perhaps we could sell it to Holt Nolan to present to the winners of his Football Challenge.'

Holt Nolan, a rich local businessman, was the owner of Muddington House. Every summer he held a fair in its grounds at which he ran a mini football competition. Muddington Colts, the junior football team that he managed, challenged any team to try to beat

21

them. So far, no team ever had: the Colts always won.

It was generally believed that Holt Nolan only held the competition as an opportunity to show off his team and to present the fancy silver trophy to his elder son, George, who was the Colts' captain. His younger son, Perry, played for the team too. He was Dan's arch-enemy at school.

Dan grasped the old ball to his chest tightly. 'No way is Perry getting this ball,' he said grimly. His parents smiled.

'Don't worry, Dan,' said Stephen Legg gently. 'No one's going to take away your ball.'

'No,' Ann Legg agreed. 'But what about this magic business?'

'Yeah!' the twins chorused. 'Do some magic, Dan!'

'I want magic! I want magic!' chanted Dan's little sister, Flora, and everyone laughed.

Dan waited until they were all quiet again. 'We aren't joking, you know,' he said very seriously. 'This ball really is magic.' He told them again about Archie's sudden and shocking appearance and the conversation that had followed.

'Now you can all meet him,' he said. He looked down at the old leather ball in his hands. 'Archie,' he said softly. 'Archie, come and meet your relatives.'

Nothing happened.

'Come on, Archie,' he pleaded. 'They're dying to meet you. Really they are.'

Still there were no ghostly stirrings . . .

'It doesn't look like Archie's dying to meet us,' said Ann Legg drily.

'Well, if he's a ghost, he'll be dead already, I suppose,' Stephen Legg remarked.

'Dad!' said Dan sternly. 'You're not taking this seriously. Archie really is . . .' He hesitated an instant. What *was* Archie? A ghost? But that sounded silly, didn't it? 'Archie is real,' he said finally.

'Yeah,' said Sam.

'He's cool,' Zak added. He glanced across at Dan. 'Maybe Sam should do what she did before,' he suggested. 'You know, that Aladdin stuff.'

Dan pulled at one ear and frowned. 'OK,' he shrugged. He handed the ball to Sam, who started to rub the ball gently.

'Arise, O Archie,' she commanded in the same quivery voice she had used in the shed earlier.

Everyone laughed again. The twins fell against each other giggling.

'Arise, O Archie,' Sam wailed once more and she rubbed the ball a little harder.

And this time, just like a genie from a magic lamp, Archie did indeed appear.

CHAPTER FIVE

ARCHIE AGAIN

Archie's second appearance was even more dramatic than his first—he came fizzing out of the ball like a firecracker. He looked more ghostly this time too. He was fuzzier at the edges and quite transparent in places.

For an instant or two there was total shocked silence as all eyes focused on the shimmering figure. Then the room erupted with voices crying out, shrieking, screaming. Flora hid her head in her mum's lap. Stephen Legg's mouth gaped open with amazement. The twins jumped up and banged heads. Dan and Sam threw up their hands in excitement. Only Zak remained calm.

It was a while before order was restored. Then Archie had to face an explosion of questions. Who was he? Was he really a ghost? How long had he been in the old ball? Was it true he was related to them? If so, how? Archie met all these questions with an indulgent smile. He stroked his big red moustache carefully, as if making sure each individual hair was in place. Then he raised a commanding hand.

'Listen and I shall tell you my story,' he said. He put his hands on his hips and waited for silence before continuing. 'My name, as I have already told these young lads here,'—he glanced with a smile at Dan, Sam and Zak—'is Archibald Legg and I believe I am indeed related to all of you in this room. I was born in 1905 and died . . . well, er, in 1938, I believe. So, yes, I am a ghost. When I was alive, I played for Muddington Rovers and, though I say it myself, I was rather good. The great Herbert Chapman, when manager of

Huddersfield Town, once offered £150 for my services.'

'£150!' Dan exclaimed and he laughed. 'Alan Shearer cost £15 million.'

'£15 million for a football player!' Archie was horrified. 'In my day you could buy every player in the world for that amount of money.' His eyes glinted and gleamed with outrage.

'He's a very good player,' Sam said gently.

'I dare say he is,' said Archie. He pushed out his chest a little. 'So was I.'

'What happened to you?' Dan asked. 'I mean, how did you die?'

'Ah,' sighed Archie. 'I was the victim of a cruel catastrophe!' His thick eyebrows joined in a bushy frown. 'One stormy day, in the winter of 1938, I was playing in a cup match for Muddington Rovers against Newcastle when suddenly, out of the blue—well, the black actually—a bolt of lightning hurtled from the sky and struck me down, just as I was about to score. I was killed immediately.'

At this terrible memory, Archie

flickered with emotion. He looked down gravely at the old football. 'This ball was the match ball that day and I have been trapped inside it ever since. I cannot tell you how delighted I am that you rescued me. I had no desire to spend the whole of my ghostly existence inhabiting a pig's bladder.'

'A pig's bladder!' cried the twins, Giles and Justin, and they squealed with laughter.

'The inside of an old football, the bit you pumped the air into, used to be made from a pig's bladder,' Stephen Legg explained.

'Gross,' said Sam.

'Yeah,' Dan agreed.

'So you've been up in the loft, inside that ball, all these years?' asked Ann Legg incredulously.

Archie nodded his large head. 'Indeed I have,' he said. 'While the ball was dead, so was I. But when these kind children revived it, I too was revived.' He gave Dan, Sam and Zak a gracious nod. 'And here I am, back in the bosom of my family.'

'Now, let me see,' mused Stephen Legg, 'judging by when you were born, you must be my grandfather's brother. My *great*-uncle.' His face flushed with excitement. 'Of course, Great-Uncle Archie!' he cried. 'I remember my grandfather talking about you. We must have a photograph of you somewhere.'

'So you're the children's great-great-uncle,' Ann Legg reflected.

'Cool,' said Zak.

Archie positively glowed with pleasure. 'Well, now that I'm here,' he said happily, 'I intend to make myself useful. I couldn't help overhearing some talk of a football challenge. That

29

wouldn't be the Football Association Challenge Trophy you were talking about, would it?' he enquired hopefully.

'Eh?' said Dan.

'He means the FA Cup,' laughed Stephen Legg. Then, turning back to Archie, he added, 'We were talking about the Holt Nolan Football Challenge.' He explained to Archie what this was.

'Oh, I see,' said Archie with some disappointment. 'Well, every team must start somewhere.'

'But what team?' said Dan. 'We don't have a team.'

'Well, there are enough of you to make a team, aren't there, laddy?' said Archie sharply. 'How many did you say you were? Fourteen, was it?'

'Yes, but . . .' Dan stammered

'You only need eleven players to form a team,' Archie persisted. 'At least that was the case in my day . . .' His eyes blazed, challenging anyone to contradict him. 'Well then, what better than to have a family team?' he declared triumphantly. 'Leggs Eleven, I shall call it.' He waggled his huge moustache thoughtfully. 'Or Leggs United, perhaps?'

Stephen Legg studied his ancestor shrewdly. 'Are you suggesting that the children form their own football team to play the Muddington Colts in the Holt Nolan Football Challenge?' he asked.

Archie nodded once vigorously, his shock of red hair flickering like fire. 'Indeed I am,' he confirmed.

'What a good idea,' said Stephen Legg with a big grin.

'Call it ghostly inspiration,' said Archie smugly.

'But the Muddington Colts are nearly all eleven or twelve,' Sam protested. She thought briefly. 'Only Dan, Zak, Rollo and Zoe are over ten.'

Archie tutted at her. 'Age is no matter in football, laddy,' he said. Then, before Sam could correct him, he continued, 'It's talent that counts—and expert management, of course.' He stared at Sam, Dan and Zak with narrowed eyes. 'And you will have a manager of unrivalled skill, experience and tactical genius.'

'We will?' said Zak.

'You will,' said Archie.

'Who?' asked Dan with a bewildered frown.

Archie puffed out his chest and raised his thick, red eyebrows. 'Why, me, of course,' he said with pride.

CHAPTER SIX

ARCHIE GETS ELECTRIC

The next afternoon, Archie held his first training session in the meadow at the bottom of the gardens of number 15 and number 17 Poplar Street. The meadow belonged to the Legg family and was the size of a large football pitch.

Sam summoned Archie from the old football and, as on each previous occasion, his appearance caused great excitement. Most of the cousins had only seen Archie once, when he had been introduced to them all the evening before, so they still found him quite astonishing. By contrast, Dan, Sam and Zak were very calm. It was weird, Dan thought, how quickly you could get used to having a ghost in the family.

'Now, before we commence training,' Archie said importantly, 'you had better tell me your names again.'

'I'm Dan,' said Dan with a grin.

'Yes, I know you,' said Archie. 'And Zak and Sam—and Miles and Julian . . .'

'*Giles* and *Justin*!' shrieked the twins together.

'Oh, yes, of course, of course,' said Archie fuzzily.

One by one the other members of the newly formed Leggs United introduced themselves: Rollo and Gabby Browne, Zak's brother and sister; then Zoe Legg and the triplets, Ben, Jack and Frances, and their little brother Billy. He was a bit young for the team, but Archie said he could join in the training.

'He can be our super sub,' said Dan.

'Super sub?' queried Archie.

'Yes' said Dan. 'Our substitute. In case anyone gets injured.'

'Substitutes aren't allowed,' said

34

Archie sternly.

'Yes they are,' said Sam. 'You're allowed three.'

'Three!' cried Archie. 'In my day, if someone got injured you played on with ten men. That was part of the excitement.' He shook his head in disbelief. 'You'll be telling me next that players can be substituted because they're not playing well enough.'

'Yes, they can,' said Sam.

'Huh?' Archie snorted. Then he tutted with disapproval. 'What would the great Herbert Chapman make of that?' His eyes narrowed to two hairy lines. 'Well, there's no *substitute* for hard work,' he declared sharply. 'So let's commence training. We'll start with some keep-ups.' He looked keenly at the group of children before him. 'Now, which of you lads is going to kick off?'

'I will,' said Sam quickly.

Archie glared at her, his bushy eyebrows bristling. 'In my day,' he said, 'girls played hockey and netball. They did not play football.'

'I do,' Sam said defiantly. 'And so do

35

my cousins.'

Archie studied Sam and Zoe in their Muddington Rovers shirts and Gabby in her goalkeeper's jersey. 'You have the clothing,' he said. 'But can you play?'

'Of course we can,' said Sam fiercely.

'They can,' Zak said. 'They're really good.' He nodded at Sam. 'Show him your keep-ups, Sam,' he urged.

Sam nodded. She flicked a football up in the air and kicked it. She trapped it on her knee and kicked it up again.

She kicked the ball with her left foot up in the air, over and over again. In all, she did twenty-five keep-ups.

'Mmm, not bad,' Archie said. He stroked his big red moustache appreciatively. Then he turned to Dan, who was smiling broadly at his sister's feats. 'Now, laddy,' said Archie. 'You show the girls how it's really done.'

Dan's smile quickly vanished. 'What?' he spluttered. 'Me?' His ears went bright red.

Archie nodded.

'But I'm a defender,' said Dan.

'Well, defenders play football, don't they?' said Archie.

'Well, yes,' said Dan doubtfully.

'Go on, then,' Archie insisted.

Reluctantly, Dan took the ball. He did five keep-ups. Then he stepped on the ball, lost his footing and fell flat on his face. The other children laughed.

'Mmm,' Archie uttered. 'Not very impressive.'

Dan got to his feet gingerly. Then he picked up the ball. He held it out to Archie. 'You show us,' he challenged.

Archie raised one eyebrow. 'Well, it

has been a long time,' he said. 'Toss the ball up, then . . .'

Dan threw the ball in the air. As it fell, Archie stuck out his right foot casually to catch it. But the ball carried on dropping, right through his foot, and bounced on the grass beneath.

Archie's eyes and mouth opened wide with astonishment. His eyebrows hopped alarmingly. 'Oh, er, well,' he said. He tried to kick the ball with his other foot. But the same thing happened. Archie scratched his head and peered down in dismay at his booted foot and then at the ball.

'It appears that I am lacking in substance,' he remarked mournfully. He looked so upset that Dan felt sorry for him.

'Maybe you just need to do some exercise,' he suggested helpfully. 'You know, to build up your strength, after all those years inside a ball.'

'Your energy level is probably low,' said Zak thoughtfully. His favourite TV programme was *The X Files* and he knew quite a lot about ghosts and the supernatural. 'I saw this programme the other night about ghosts and electricity,' he continued. 'When a ghost is near electricity it gets more energy and its body gets more, well, solid—like ours.'

'Maybe Archie should put his finger in an electric socket,' said Sam.

Archie frowned. 'I've already been electrocuted once, thank you,' he rasped. 'I have no desire to repeat the experience.'

Zak shook his head. 'No,' he said. 'It's more a question of trying to draw the waves of electricity in from around you, I think. You know, think electric.'

'Think electric?' Archie queried, his big moustache twitching. 'I don't understand what you mean.'

'I get it!' said Dan excitedly. He pointed to a garden nearby where a man was cutting his grass. 'See that electric lawnmower, Archie,' he said. 'Think of the power that's surging through it. Try and draw some of that power into your body.'

Archie still looked completely bemused, but he did as Dan suggested. For about thirty seconds, he stared at the lawnmower with deep concentration. Then he sighed. 'I cannot feel a thing,' he said sadly.

'Try again,' Zak urged. 'Really concentrate.'

'Go on, Archie!' the twins chorused as one.

Once more, Archie focused on the lawnmower. He stood completely silent, eyes staring, head and body completely still—and the children stood still and silent too, watching him.

For several seconds, nothing happened. Then, all of a sudden, there was a hiss and a fizz and Archie's shock of red hair seemed to blaze from his head. The faint glimmer that surrounded him became a dazzling light: Archie quivered and shone.

When he turned to face the children again, his face was beaming.

'I feel as if lightning has struck for a second time,' he announced happily. 'But this time it's brought me to life.'

He aimed a kick at the old football. It zipped away through the air and thudded against the wall, scaring a fat crow that was sitting there.

'Now,' Archie declared, 'that is more like it.'

CHAPTER SEVEN

GHOSTLY GOALIE

Over the next few days, Archie spent a lot of time practising drawing electricity into his body—with increasing success. His energy levels shot up amazingly. He became a ghostly dynamo and worked his team very hard. Every morning they had a long training session that started with a run around the meadow and ended with a short six-a-side game.

In between, Archie taught the children a variety of skills. He showed them how to dribble and bodyswerve, how to nutmeg and sell a dummy, how to volley and bend a shot like a banana.

They practised trapping the ball, passing, shielding, tackling and, of course, keep-ups.

'You must learn to be the ball's master and not the reverse,' Archie told his players. 'As the great Herbert Chapman once said, "Control the ball and you control the match."'

Archie mentioned Herbert Chapman a lot and always with deep respect. In Archie's opinion, Herbert Chapman was the greatest manager that had ever lived. He won the championship twice in a row with Huddersfield Town and was on the verge of achieving the same feat with Arsenal when he died, suddenly, of pneumonia.

Recalling his hero's death, Archie shimmered with emotion. He actually looked for an instant as if he might burst into tears. His moustache quivered and his eyebrows trembled. Then he took a deep breath and steadied himself.

'Right, on with the training,' he commanded. 'Ball skills. Dan, toss a ball up.'

Just as he had a few days before, Dan

threw a ball in the air. Once again, as the ball dropped, Archie stuck out his right foot to catch it. The children watched, breath held, wondering what would happen . . .

This time the ball landed on Archie's foot and stayed there. He held it for a moment then, with a contented smile, he flicked the ball up again and caught it on his left foot. He juggled the ball from foot to foot, then from knee to bony knee. Then he bounced the ball on his head, eventually letting it roll down his back and over his bottom. When it reached his calf he kicked up his heel and flicked the ball back over his head and into his hands.

'Wow!' said Dan.

'Cool,' said Zak.

'Do it again!' demanded the twins. So Archie did. This time he balanced the ball on top of his head, before allowing it to slide down his back. When he'd finished, everyone clapped.

Archie glowed so much that his hair looked as if it was on fire. 'Thank you, thank you. You're too kind,' he said happily.

The children were constantly amazed by Archie's football skills. It seemed as if he could do anything. He could even play in goal. Gabby was the Leggs United goalie. She wasn't very tall but she was a very good gymnast and had an amazing spring. After Thursday's training session, Archie gave her some extra coaching. Dan, Sam and Zak stayed behind to watch. Archie showed Gabby how to come out and narrow the angle when faced with an attacker, where to stand for corners, and lots of other useful tips.

'I'll tell you a little goalkeeper's trick,' he said with a theatrical wink, as if he were passing on some priceless secret. 'When I played in goal, I used to make a little mark at the centre of the six-yard line to help me get my positioning right.'

'Were you a goalkeeper then?' Gabby asked, puzzled. 'I thought you were a forward.'

'Ah, yes, indeed I was,' said Archie. 'But I often took a turn in goal in practice matches and on a few occasions, when our goalkeeper was injured, I was called upon to take his place.' He smiled smugly. 'I was rather good, too,' he declared, 'though I say it myself.' The cousins raised their eyes and groaned.

As if to prove the point, Archie went in goal and invited Dan, Sam and Zak to take shots at him.

The ghostly goalie proved quite impossible to beat. He leapt and dived in a fiery flash that took him from side to side, up and down. He saved everything.

'How do you do that?' Dan marvelled, as Archie plucked yet another goalbound shot from the air.

'Yeah, that was cool,' Zak agreed.

'Call it phantom power,' Archie replied mysteriously, tapping his long nose with a bony finger.

Gabby looked rather disheartened. 'I'll never be as good as you,' she said flatly, her shoulders drooping.

'Nonsense, nonsense,' Archie retorted quickly with a waggle of his huge moustache. 'You'll be just fine. I've not seen such an agile young keeper since the great Frank Swift was a lad.' This compliment was met by bemused silence.

'Who's Frank Swift?' Sam asked at last.

'Who's Frank Swift?' Archie repeated incredulously. 'Who's Frank Swift? Why, only the best goalkeeper of his age.' He threw up his large hands dramatically. 'Indeed, of any age, I should venture,' he added.

'What, better than you?' said Dan mischievously.

Archie grinned broadly. 'Well, let's say he was one of the two best keepers of his age,' he said.

CHAPTER EIGHT

THE INVISIBLE MANAGER

On Friday, the day before the Summer Fair, Archie spent most of his final training session talking tactics. He sorted out the team positions and the formation he wanted them to play. This was the line-up:

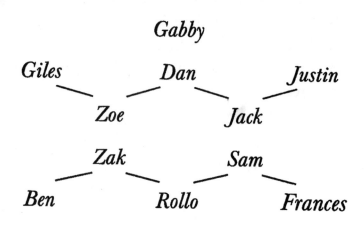

Gabby

Giles   *Dan*   *Justin*

     Zoe   *Jack*

     Zak   *Sam*

Ben   *Rollo*   *Frances*

'Is that 3–2–2–3?' asked Dan.

'I suppose you could say so,' said Archie. 'It was Herbert Chapman's invention, the WM formation. It made Arsenal the greatest team in the world.' He gazed upwards with an odd, dreamy look. 'Hulme, Bastin, Lambert, Jack and James—what a forward line.'

'Muddington Rovers play 3–5–2,' said Sam.

Archie's expression turned from admiration to disapproval. 'Do they indeed?' he sniffed. 'However do they score any goals with only two forwards?'

'They don't very often,' said Zak glumly. Muddington Rovers had been relegated the season before.

'Well, there you are, then,' said Archie huffily. He put his hands on his hips and fixed his team with a fizzing stare. '*We* are going to score lots of goals, are we not, Leggs United?'

'Yes!' came the unanimous reply.

'Good,' said Archie.

'And we're not going to let any in,' said Dan determinedly.

'I should think not,' agreed Archie.

'Not with you at the heart of our defence.' He paused a moment before continuing, with a nod at Gabby, 'And with young Frank Swift there in goal, of course.'

Gabby smiled. 'I'll do my best,' she said eagerly.

'That's all anyone can do,' said Archie. 'It's the spirit that counts.' He stroked his moustache proudly and put one foot on the old ball. 'And when that spirit is Archibald Legg,' he declared, 'the opposition had better beware!'

At that moment, as if on cue, a horn blared, announcing the arrival of Perry and George Nolan. They were on their bikes, looking over the wall across the meadow. As the assembled Leggs and Brownes turned round, Perry sounded his horn once more.

'Up the Colts!' he cried.

Dan greeted his enemy with a hostile scowl. 'What do you want?' he called fiercely.

'We just stopped by to size up the opposition,' said George, smirking.

'Yeah, we heard you're entering the Challenge tomorrow,' said Perry. He

jerked his head at Dan and sneered.
'You'll thrash you,' he boasted.

'Says who?' Dan replied.

'Says anyone with half a brain.'
George goaded.

'Hear that, Archie?' said Dan,
turning to his manager, who was still
standing with one foot on the old ball.

'Indeed, I did,' Archie replied coolly.
'Take no notice. We'll do our talking on
the field of play.'

'What's that, then—your lucky
mascot?' Perry said, nodding at the old
ball.

'Archie!' scoffed George. 'Funny

name for a ball.' The two brothers sniggered.

'He wasn't talking to the ball, you idiots,' Sam hissed. 'He was talking to our manager, Archie. He used to play for Muddington Rovers.'

Archie raised his head and smiled smugly.

'I don't see anyone,' said Perry, looking around with a baffled expression.

'Yeah, where is he then, this Archie?' demanded George.

'There, you wallies,' said Dan, pointing at Archie.

'What are you talking about?' said George. 'There's no one there—just an old ball.'

Dan frowned and tugged at his ear. He was the one looking baffled now.

'You can't see Archie?' he said. 'He's standing right there with his foot on the ball.'

'You're nuts,' said Perry. 'There's no one there.' He studied the Leggs contemptuously. Then his face suddenly screwed up in disgust. 'You've got girls in your team!' he cried.

'You really will need a lucky mascot,' laughed George. 'Come on, Perry,' he said, 'let's go and tell the others the good news. Leggs United are rubbish. And they're bonkers!'

'Yeah,' said Perry. The two got back on their bikes and turned to go.

'See you Saturday, suckers!' shouted Perry as the brothers cycled away.

For a few moments, there was silence in the meadow. Then Dan said quietly, 'They couldn't see you, Archie.'

'It seems not,' Archie agreed, frowning sadly.

There was another moment's silence, then Zak spoke up. 'Maybe only your relatives can see you,' he suggested.

'What do you mean?' asked Dan.

'That happens sometimes with ghosts,' said Zack. 'I read about it in a book.'

Archie pondered this idea with a slow caress of his moustache. 'Well, as long as *you* can see me, I suppose that is all that matters,' he said at last. He looked in the direction the Nolan brothers had taken. 'They'll see my genius in action soon enough . . .'

CHAPTER NINE

SURPRISE SURPRISE

On Saturday morning, Dan was woken by an excited Sam. She was hopping up and down at his bedside, shouting something about a surprise. 'Come downstairs!' she cried. 'Come and see!'

Dan yawned and rubbed his eyes. Then he rolled out of bed and shuffled downstairs after his sister. 'What is it?' he asked sleepily.

And then he saw. His eyes popped open. Suddenly he was wide awake.

'Wow!' he uttered. In front of him stood Sam and the twins, each wearing a smart new football shirt, with red and white squares and the words *Legg's*

Motors across the front. Behind the children, holding up an identical shirt, was their uncle Mark.

'How do you like your new team strip, Dan?' he asked, passing Dan the shirt in his hands. Dan stared at the new shirt, then he looked at his sister and brothers.

'It's brilliant,' he said.

'Look at the back,' said Sam. Dan turned the shirt round. On the back was a black number 5 and his name.

'Cool,' he said, delighted. He pulled the shirt on over his pyjama top and then ran off to look at himself in the mirror. The others followed him.

'Thanks, Uncle Mark,' Dan said, when he'd finally finished admiring himself. 'It's really great.'

'Well, you can't be a proper team without a proper kit, can you?' Mark Legg shrugged. 'Besides, it's good advertising for my garage.' He grinned and touched the silver ring in his ear. 'Well, as long as you win, of course.'

'Don't worry, we'll win,' said Dan airily.

Later, however, when they got to the

fair, he didn't feel quite so confident. Holt Nolan's Football Challenge had already begun. Two other teams, besides Leggs United, had entered. Each game was to last 40 minutes; 20 minutes each way. In the first game the Colts had thrashed their opponents ten-nil, and they were now playing—and easily beating—the second team.

Dan and the rest of his team arrived just as Perry Nolan scored to give the Colts a 4–1 lead. The goal was a simple tap-in, but the way Perry celebrated, you'd have thought it had been something really spectacular. He leapt in the air and shouted, then dived across the pitch like an Olympic swimmer.

'Show-off,' Daniel tutted. 'Wait till he's facing me. I'll show him.'

'Careful, though,' said Zak. 'Don't forget, his dad's the ref.' He nodded across at Holt Nolan, who was standing in the middle of the pitch with a whistle round his neck and a smile about ten metres wide.

Dan humphed. 'Like father, like son,' he said grimly. Then he looked down at

56

the old ball he was cradling in his arms. 'I think it's time we called Archie,' he said.

Archie was a little confused at first. He looked fuzzier than ever; almost as if he'd been sketched on the air with a blunt pencil, Dan thought. He glanced about, checking to see if anyone had noticed the phantom footballer's arrival. No one had. Several people walked by without batting an eyelid. It seemed, then, that what Zak had suggested was true: Archie was only visible to his family.

'Where am I?' Archie asked groggily. 'What is all this?' He peered around blearily at all the people and the stalls, at one of which the adult Leggs were now busy selling their wares. 'Is this Wembley Stadium?'

'You're at the Muddington House Summer Fair,' Sam informed him.

'For the Holt Nolan Football Challenge,' Zak added.

'We're on next,' said Dan. He gestured to where the Muddington Colts were celebrating yet another goal. The game was almost over now and there was no doubt who was going to win.

'Ah, yes, of course, of course, the Challenge,' Archie muttered. 'When you woke me I was playing in the Cup Final. I'd just scored a wonderful goal. Frank Swift never had a chance.' He grinned hazily at the memory.

'Do ghosts have dreams then?' Dan asked. It seemed an odd idea to him.

'Of course we do,' snorted Archie. 'It would be a dull old life if we didn't.' His moustache wiggled, as if something was not quite right. 'Well, a dull old death, if you see what I mean,' he added.

He looked around at his players, glowing with proud satisfaction as he took in their smart new strip. 'Right, there's no time to lose. I'll just get myself charged up and then we shall have our final team talk . . .' He started focusing on a generator which was powering a nearby bouncy castle.

A few minutes later, as Archie and Dan were talking about corner tactics, two opposition players joined the Leggs on the touchline. It was Perry and George Nolan, fresh from their recent

victory.

'Still talking to that old ball?' Perry jeered. 'Oh, sorry, I mean your manager.' He turned to George and they both sniggered.

'Just ignore them,' said Archie calmly. 'Stay cool.'

'You'll be laughing on the other side of your face when we beat you,' said Dan defiantly.

'You've got no chance,' Perry scoffed. 'My dad's offered to donate £500 to Muddington Primary if we lose.'

'So?' said Dan.

'Dad never gives away money to anyone,' said George with a knowing grin.

'*And* he's the ref,' Perry added, smirking.

George Nolan gave the magic ball a rude prod with his foot. 'Hello, anyone in there?'

Archie could take no more. His calm ignited into fury. He hopped up and down and shouted, 'Hoodlum! Whippersnapper!' He gave the Nolan brothers such a fiery glare that some of the younger Leggs shrank back in alarm. But not George and Perry Nolan. After all, they couldn't see or hear Archie, could they?

'See you on the pitch,' said Perry casually.

'Yeah, for the slaughter,' added George. Then the two brothers walked away, sneering.

Now Archie was really fuming. He waved his fist at the departing Colts. 'Mock Archibald Legg, would you?' he snarled. Then he turned to face his team with an expression of wild determination. 'Right, Leggs United,' he declared. 'This is war!'

CHAPTER TEN

ARCHIE EXPLODES

The match started well for Leggs United; after just two minutes, they took the lead. Dan booted the ball upfield; Sam trapped it neatly on her chest and flicked a pass across to Zak. Taking the ball in his stride, Zak swerved past George Nolan and lashed the ball into the net.

The Colts looked stunned. After their two easy wins, this wasn't at all what they'd expected. Reluctantly, Holt Nolan blew his whistle and pointed back to the centre. Then he gave his oldest son a severe telling-off for letting Zak get past him.

On the touchline, the adult Leggs clapped and cheered.

'Great goal, team!' shouted Stephen Legg.

'Let's have another,' Mark Legg added.

'Nice one, son,' called Zak's dad, Otis Browne, giving a thumbs-up sign.

Archie hardly moved a muscle. He stood quite still with his arms folded, one foot on the magic ball, as if posing for a photo. His face bore a look of calm contentment. Everything appeared to be going perfectly to plan.

It didn't last long, however. Less than a minute later, Leggs United were in trouble. Perry Nolan's striking partner, Matt Blake, ran between Jack and Justin and then knocked the ball through Dan's legs as he came across to tackle. Gabby came out to narrow the angle, as Archie had shown her, but Matt was too quick. He flicked the ball past her towards the goal. It was just about to roll over the line and into the net, when Perry raced forward and threw himself at the ball, so that he could claim the goal for himself. Once again, he celebrated like he'd scored the goal of the season.

Dan felt sick. He was cross with himself for falling for Matt's nutmeg trick and fed up that it was Perry who'd scored. But worse was soon to follow. In their next attack, the Colts got a corner kick and Rollo headed the ball into his own goal. From being a goal up, Leggs United were 2–1 down!

For the rest of the first half, the Colts were well on top. The ball was hardly out of the Leggs' half. Archie's tactic of booting the ball down the wings for Frances and Ben to chase just wasn't working. Both were very fast runners for their age, but they were up against defenders who were three years older than them. Only Gabby's brilliant goal-keeping and some timely tackles by Dan kept Leggs United in the match.

It was no surprise when the Colts scored a third goal. It came after one of Leggs United's rare attacks. In the excitement of finally getting the ball into their opponents' penalty area, Zoe and Jack rushed upfield to support the front five players. As one, the twins went chasing after them. When the attack came to nothing and the Colts' goalie booted the ball clear, only Dan was left in defence against both Perry Nolan and Matt Blake.

The ball ran to Perry, but he didn't trap it cleanly. Seeing his chance, Dan moved across and tackled his enemy. It was a good tackle but, unluckily for Dan, the ball bounced away off Perry's shin straight into the path of Matt Blake.

Once again, Gabby came out to narrow the angle. This time, she managed to get a hand to Matt's shot, but she couldn't stop it going into the net. 3–1 to the Colts!

Archie's cool turned to rage. As the Colts celebrated, he burst onto the pitch like a wild fire. His target was Holt Nolan.

'Offside!' he exploded at the referee, his face red with fury. 'Are you blind, you fool? Don't you know the rules? That was offside by a mile!'

The Leggs players and supporters turned and stared in astonishment at Archie, who was now waving his fists at Holt Nolan. It looked as if he was about to punch him on the nose.

'Archie!' Stephen Legg cried. 'What are you doing? Get off the pitch.'

Archie turned and glowered at his relative. 'It was offside,' Archie repeated angrily. 'Didn't you see?'

'The rules have changed, Archie,' Zak explained soothingly. 'Matt was standing in line with Dan. That's not offside now. Really. It was a fair goal.'

Archie greeted this information with

65

a thunderous scowl, but he did leave the pitch. He gave Holt Nolan a scorching glare, growled something under his breath and then marched back to the touchline. His outline pulsed with rage.

Holt Nolan, meanwhile, had trotted back to the centre and the Muddington Colts had lined up for the kick-off. A few of them pointed at Zak and shook their heads in amusement. As far as they could see, he was explaining the rules of football to thin air!

Holt Nolan peeped his whistle. 'Are you still in this game, Leggs United?' he shouted impatiently.

'Come on, Leggs United!' Mark Legg urged from the touchline.

The Leggs players turned and gaped at one another uncertainly. They hadn't moved since Archie's outburst and looked as if they were in a dream, awaiting their manager's instructions. But Archie was too busy fuming to give any orders. It was up to the captain, Dan, to wake his team up. He clapped his hands sharply.

'Let's go, team!' he cried. Then he ran back to take up his place in defence.

'Doesn't look like your lucky ball's working,' Perry sneered as Dan jogged past him.

'The game's not over yet,' Dan flung back defiantly.

But in his heart, he feared it might be.

CHAPTER ELEVEN

A CHANGE OF TACTICS

Half-time came at last. The score was still 3–1 to the Colts, but only because Perry Nolan missed an open goal. Just a couple of metres out, with Gabby on the ground, Perry decided to blast the ball when all he had to do was tap it over the line. The ball thundered against the post and rebounded straight into his stomach, knocking him flat. He writhed around and groaned like a snake with bellyache. Holt Nolan blew his whistle.

'Half-time,' he called, running over to his felled son.

Normally Dan would have laughed at

Perry's antics, but not now. He trooped off the pitch, glumly, with the rest of the Leggs.

'Well tried, team,' Stephen Legg said encouragingly.

'Yes, there's still another half to go,' Mark Legg pointed out.

'Hmm,' Dan uttered gloomily. Another half like the one they'd just had wasn't much to look forward to. What would Archie say about what had happened?

As it turned out, Archie was now surprisingly calm and at ease. He'd cooled down once more and was sitting on the old ball, stroking his moustache thoughtfully.

'I see things are a little different from in my day,' he reflected. His eyebrows hopped critically. 'Not better, certainly not, but different. A few tactical changes are in order, I believe.'

The main problem, Archie said, was that the defence and attack were too far apart. The long ball over the top of the Colts' defence wasn't working at all and the front W was playing too flat. The system needed tweaking. So, while

Zak's mum, Julia Browne, handed round drinks to the team, Archie made some tactical changes.

For the second half, Leggs United would line up with the same WM formation, but now Jack and Rollo would play in front of the defence, with Sam and Zoe pairing up behind the forwards Zak, Frances and Ben.

The new arrangement would look like this:

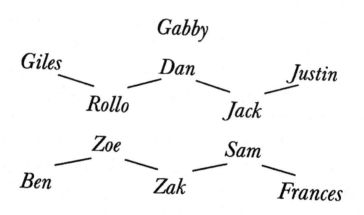

'You two are the linkmen,' Archie told Sam and Zoe. 'You have to link defence and attack—the role I often played myself for Muddington Rovers.' He smiled proudly.

'Link *girls*, you mean,' said Sam,

frowning indignantly from under her fringe.

Archie's smile became a steely glare. 'You may be girls,' he said sternly, 'but I expect you to play like men. The success of our attacks depends upon you.'

'Huh,' Sam snorted. 'We'll show you how we can play.'

Archie told Dan to stay close to Matt Blake and not allow him any room on the ball. 'Stop him and you stop the Colts,' he declared with a flamboyant waggle of his moustache. 'It's as simple as that. Now, go out and win!'

Archie's confidence rubbed off on his team. They took the field for the second half with spirits lifted. From the whistle, they went on the attack and, as in the first half, they scored an early goal.

The move began with Sam. She got the ball in midfield and weaved past two defenders before sliding the ball down the wing. For once, Ben had lots of space and no defender near him. He raced along the wing to the goal line and sent over a teasing cross. The goalkeeper stretched but could only push the ball into the path of Zak, who slammed it into the net. 3–2 and Leggs United were back in the match!

As Leggs United found new energy, the Colts began to tire. This was, after all, their third game of the day. Perry Nolan was puffing and panting, while Matt Blake couldn't get away from Dan at all. For about the tenth time in the half, Dan took the ball off the Colts' striker and fed it through to Rollo. On it went to Zoe. She was tackled by George Nolan but the ball ran to Sam. A quick sprint forward, a swerving shot, and the ball was in the Colts' net for the equalizer.

'Great goal, Sam!' shouted the adult Leggs, applauding heartily.

Sam glanced across at Archie. 'Not bad for a girl, eh?' she called.

Archie raised his hairy eyebrows and nodded with approval. He was the picture of contentment once more.

It seemed only a matter of time now before Leggs United would score again—with Sam really enjoying her playmaking role and Zak a constant threat upfront. The Muddington Colts looked dead on their feet. The game was all being played in their half.

But the goal wouldn't come. Zak went close twice, Ben hit a post and then Sam had a goal disallowed by Holt Nolan for offside.

'No way!' she cried, furious at the decision.

'The referee's decision is final,' said Holt Nolan smugly.

'Hey, stay cool,' Zak told Sam. 'We'll get another chance.'

He was right. With just minutes left, Leggs United finally got the breakthrough their play deserved. George Nolan hit a weak back pass. Quick as a flash, Zak ran on to it, flicked the ball past the goalie and banged the ball into the net. There was nothing Holt Nolan could do this time, except blow his whistle to signal a goal. Zak had his hat-kick and Leggs United were in the lead!

Now Archie did get excited. He leapt up and did a little jig, his bony white knees pumping up and down in a ghostly whirr. Dan laughed. The

spectating Leggs cheered. Like Archie, they thought the game was all over. But the Nolan family had other ideas.

A last desperate clearance from the Colts bounced deep into the Leggs United half. Perry Nolan chased after it. Dan made no attempt to follow. It was a hopeless chase because Gabby was going to beat Perry to the ball quite easily. Still Perry carried on running. The ball rolled into Gabby's arms. She collected it and stood up—just as Perry arrived. He ran right up to her and threw himself to the ground as if he'd been tripped. It was the most outrageous dive Dan had ever seen. No referee could fall for that, surely?

But then Holt Nolan wasn't just the referee, was he? He was also the manager of Muddington Colts and Perry's dad too. He blew his whistle at once.

'Penalty kick!' he cried and, to everyone's disbelief, he pointed to the spot.

CHAPTER TWELVE

ARCHIE LENDS A FOOT

Once more, Archie exploded on to the pitch. As Holt Nolan ran into the Leggs United penalty area, Archie rushed at him, arms aloft, fists shaking, blazing with energy as if he'd just consumed an electricity pylon.

'Cheat!' he shouted. 'Dirty swizzler! This is the most disgraceful refereeing display since that fool Harper ruined the 1932 Cup Final!'

Holt Nolan might not have been able to see or hear Archie, but he could feel him. Archie shoved him and sent him stumbling backwards. The Colts' manager cried out in surprise and looked down at his chest, where Archie's hands had touched him. Then he glanced about with a baffled expression.

After a moment or two, he shrugged and, collecting himself, strode forward again, straight past Archie, who was still pulsing with anger.

'It's amazing,' Dan said to Zak. 'The Colts *still* can't see Archie, even when he's glowing like that.'

'They can see the ball and the goal, though,' Zak pointed out dolefully. He nodded at Perry, who was preparing to take the penalty. 'We don't need a ghost—we need a miracle,' he muttered from behind a drooping mop of hair.

'Gabby might save the penalty,' Dan said hopefully, pulling nervously on one ear. He didn't really feel very hopeful. His cousin was a good goalie, but she wasn't used to facing penalty kicks. Perry practised taking them a lot. He was always boasting about how good he was at penalties. If he scored, the game would end in a draw and that meant that the Colts, as champions, would keep the Challenge Trophy.

But Archie had not given up. While the Leggs United players lined up dejectedly at the edge of the penalty area, he bustled into the goal beside Gabby. He studied Perry Nolan for an instant with a keen eye.

'Feint to go left, then dive to your right,' he instructed.

'How do you know he'll shoot that way?' Gabby asked.

'Call it ghost's intuition,' Archie replied mysteriously. He stepped back behind the goal line, arms folded.

Gabby shrugged. 'OK,' she said. She swayed from side to side, getting ready to face Perry's kick.

Perry grinned triumphantly at the Leggs United players, most of whom had their heads down, unable to watch. But not Dan. He glared back at his enemy defiantly. The whistle blew. Perry raced forward and thumped the ball towards the corner of the net.

As soon as he'd hit the ball, he leapt in the air, certain he'd sent Gabby the wrong way. In fact, he'd already spun around to receive his team-mates' congratulations when Gabby reached the ball and pushed it past her right-hand post.

Now it was the Leggs' turn to celebrate. They shouted and jumped in the air and hugged one another. Off the pitch, the adults did the same. Dan ran over to Gabby and they slapped hands in a high five.

'David Seaman, eat your heart out,' Dan said excitedly.

Still standing behind the goal line, Archie grinned like a manager who'd just pulled off a master stroke. 'Frank

Swift could not have done better,' he remarked happily.

A blast of Holt Nolan's whistle brought the Leggs United's celebrations to a sudden end. 'The goalkeeper moved before the kick,' Holt Nolan declared. 'The penalty must be retaken.'

Dan stared at the referee in total astonishment. 'What?' he cried.

Zak, who knew the rules inside out, quickly came to his friend's support. 'But that rule changed in 1997,' he protested. 'She's allowed to move, as long as she stays on her line.'

Holt Nolan shook his head. 'Don't argue with the referee, sonny,' he said. 'That's the oldest rule in the book.' Then before Zak could comment, he went on, 'The kick's got to be retaken and that's final. This is my competition and you do what I say.'

Archie met this latest injustice with glowering contempt.

'So that's the way you want to play it, sir, is it?' he growled. Then he ordered everyone except Gabby out of the penalty area.

'There is no use in arguing with this petty chiseller,' he said. 'Do as he says.'

'What about me?' Gabby asked. 'Which way should I go this time?'

Archie pursed his lips. 'Neither way,' he said. 'Stay exactly where you are.'

'But if he puts it to either side, he'll score,' Gabby said.

'Trust me. Don't move,' Archie insisted. He tapped his long nose. 'We ghosts know about these things.' He closed his eyes and frowned as if in deep concentration.

Once again, the ball was put on the penalty spot. Holt Nolan blew his whistle. Perry sprinted forward and kicked the ball. This time, though, he kicked the ground as well and scuffed his shot. The ball rolled towards the line, nearer to the centre of the goal than the corner. All Gabby had to do to make a save was take a few steps to her right. But she didn't. She stood right where she was, just as Archie had commanded her. Dan watched, helpless and horrified, with the rest of his team, as the ball trickled towards the goal line . . .

'Move, Gabby!' squealed the twins. 'Move!'

But Gabby didn't move—and anyway now it was too late. The ball was about to cross the line. It was a certain goal.

There are two different views as to what happened next. In the eyes of Holt Nolan and his team, an incredible, freak event occurred: as the ball reached the goal line, it hit a hidden bump and changed direction, bobbling away from the goal and round the post.

What the Leggs United players and supporters saw was quite different. They saw the ball roll towards the line and the steel toe cap of an old boot shoot out to flick it away. They even saw the huge grin on the phantom footballer's face after he made the save.

Whichever view you choose to accept, the result was the same. The penalty was missed and Leggs United had won!

CHAPTER THIRTEEN

SWEET DREAMS

'We won the cup, we won the cup, ee-aye-addio, we won the cup!'

It was Saturday evening and Sam was dancing round the kitchen, singing, with Holt Nolan's Football Challenge Trophy on her head. She was still dressed in her Leggs United strip.

'Hey, watch out you don't drop it,' said Dan, with an anxious tug of his ear. He still couldn't quite believe that the trophy was theirs, that they'd actually beaten the Muddington Colts. It was just too amazing. He smiled as he recalled the sour look on George and Perry Nolan's faces when he walked forward to collect the trophy. Their dad looked pretty sick too. But then they deserved to feel bad. 'Cheats never prosper,' as Stephen Legg had remarked on the way home.

It had been a great day for the Legg family. Leggs United had won the Holt Nolan Trophy and Ann Legg's stall had been a big success and raised lots of money for Muddington Primary. Moreover, Holt Nolan had had to donate £500 to the school. He had not been happy.

'It was brilliant, wasn't it?' Sam said now, her freckly face bright with happiness. She plonked down on to a chair, her fringe flopping over her eyes, and put the trophy onto the table next to the old ball.

'Yeah,' Dan sighed. 'It was.'

He gazed lovingly at the trophy for a minute or so, then he turned his gaze to the old ball. A week ago it had lain flat and forgotten in the loft with Archie trapped inside it. So much had happened in the days since then, he thought, that it was impossible now to imagine life without Archie.

'Let's call Archie,' Dan said. 'I'd like to thank him.'

Sam nodded. 'We couldn't have done it without Archie,' she agreed. She leant forward and picked up the old ball. Then rubbing it gently, she began the familiar wail.

'Arise, O Archie,' she chanted. 'Archie, arise.'

An instant later, Archie fizzed out in front of them, glowing gently in the murky evening light. Dan took in once again the shock of red hair, wild eyebrows, huge walrus moustache, the old Muddington Rovers football strip with long, baggy shorts, bulky shinpads and heavy boots, the bandy legs and white, almost transparent kneecaps, the knotted neckerchief . . .

'We just wanted to thank you,' Dan greeted his ghostly relative. 'On behalf of the whole team.'

'Yes, thanks, Archie,' Sam said. 'You're the best manager in the whole world.'

Archie's pale, shimmering face coloured a little and his moustache wrinkled. 'Thank you, thank you. You're not so bad yourself,' he said good-humouredly. 'For a girl.'

'Cheers,' Sam said with a big grin.

'Thanks for the helping foot too,' said Dan. 'We needed that.'

'Yes,' said Sam. 'You were truly electric.'

'Foot? What foot?' Archie queried, all innocence. 'The ball hit a bobble. Wasn't that the referee's official verdict?' His face screwed up into an expression of deep distaste. 'I cannot

86

abide cheats,' he hissed. 'That game was won fair and square.'

'Yeah, it was never a penalty,' said Sam.

'Indeed, it wasn't,' Archie said. 'That's why I did what I did. It was a matter of justice.' His expression relaxed into a blissful sigh. 'Anyway,' he continued, 'I believe my tactical genius bamboozled them.'

'Those tactical changes certainly worked a treat,' said Dan.

'Yes,' agreed Archie. 'The WM formation may have its critics, but to me it is proof of Herbert Chapman's genius. Next time, I'm sure, we shall get it right from the start.'

Dan frowned. 'Next time?' he enquired. 'What next time?'

'Next time you play,' said Archie casually.

'When's that, then?' asked Sam, intrigued.

'In a short while, when the new season commences,' Archie informed them. 'Your father has agreed to enter you in a local league. The same one, I believe, that the Muddington Colts play in.' His eyebrows rose artfully.

'Wow,' said Dan.

'Great!' cried Sam.

'Indeed,' said Archie. 'And now, I must return to my pig's bladder to repose. It's been a very tiring week for an old ghost.' He yawned. 'Tomorrow we can commence planning for the great challenge ahead.' He raised a large, bony hand in farewell. 'Goodnight, sweet dreams,' he muttered. And with these words, the tired but triumphant Leggs United manager began to fade, dematerializing into the old ball.

'Goodnight, Archie,' said Dan. 'Sleep tight.'

'Watch out the bugs don't bite,' Sam added warmly.

Then the two children stood in silence, staring at the faint glow in the air left by the phantom footballer, until it had vanished entirely.